MIS~~~~NG

L. F. Gobin

MOVING HOUSE

"Do we have to move, Mum?" I complained yet again. Mum sighed impatiently, obviously fed up with me asking the same question.

"For the thousandth time, I have no choice. Since your dad left, it's down to me to make ends meet."

She had been promoted and had to move to another branch at the bank. I knew it wasn't her fault and I knew we had to move. Dad had left us and that was that. They had been having problems for a while and at one point the arguments had gotten really bad. Then one day, Dad told Mum he'd had enough and he moved out. We were on our own. Mum couldn't rely on Dad for money – he was always in and out of work. Mum was the one who made sure the bills were paid and that there was food on the table. I knew about the sacrifices that she had made, yet I was still annoyed, and didn't want her to know that I knew she had made the right decision. I decided to sulk in silence.

"I think you'll love it, JD. We'll be right next to a huge park where there are deer. I know you like wildlife. We'll have a larger house and you'll make new friends too."

I just answered with a shrug of my shoulders. Mum's greying, brown hair swung into her eyes as she shook her head disappointedly. She left me to it and got on with getting dinner ready. I went to my small, cosy bedroom, decorated just the way I wanted it – glow in the dark stars on the ceiling, blue walls and matching blue furniture. It's like we were starting from scratch. We would have to redecorate the new place. Mum said that the walls were magnolia. Magnolia. The most boring, generic colour ever.

I reluctantly started packing my belongings, as well as sorting out what we were giving away to charity. I came across a ring that belonged to my grandmother. It was a simple design made from what looked like twisted silver wire. She gave it to me before she died last year. I never wore it, even though it fitted me. I put it on, feeling oddly comforted by it. It shimmered in the waning light.

"JD? Dinner's ready!" Mum called. Realising how hungry I was, I eagerly ran to the living room.

After dinner, I sat on my bed in silence ready for my last day at school tomorrow, listening to the clock ticking and trying to reassure myself that I would keep in touch with my friends and see them again. After all, I wasn't moving to another country. My things were strewn around the room and I made a mental note to finish packing them tonight, ready for tomorrow.

It turned out to be yet *another* crazy morning. As soon as I said goodbye to Mum, I rushed down our street with a piece of toast half hanging out of my mouth. I didn't want to be late on my last day, as it was the last time I would be going to Springbrook Primary School. Not only was I going to miss my class, but I was also going to miss my form teacher, Mr. Trudell. He was the kindest and funniest teacher I'd ever had. I stumbled into class a few minutes late.

"Almost saved by the bell again I see, Jaden," commented Mr. Trudell as I walked in. I could hear stifled giggles as I sat at my table.

"Sorry, sir, I..."

"You didn't hear your alarm? You missed the bus? You forgot your packed lunch?"

I could feel my cheeks reddening with embarrassment. I didn't bother trying to come up with an excuse. He had heard them all. And he knew I hated when people called me by my real name too.

"Hey. Happy last day," my friend Shanice whispered.

"Thanks."

The rest of the day was a blur and before I knew it, it was three-thirty and time to leave. I said a quick goodbye to my friends and managed not to break down into a blubbering mess. I quickly left before the tears came. I felt silly for feeling so upset. I tapped my pocket as I walked home to double-check that I had my notebook containing my friends' contact details.

Mum was busy carrying boxes into the living room when I arrived home.

"How was your last day, love?"

"It was fine," I said brusquely, not wanting to talk about it. I went straight to my room to finish packing.

A tanned face framed with dark hair looked back at me in the bathroom mirror. My hazel eyes looked sad. Big move day had arrived. The removal van was parked outside and almost everything had been loaded. I took one last look around my room and I noticed something shimmering on the floor. It was Grandma's ring. I had almost left it! I hurriedly picked it up and put it on my finger.

We arrived at our new house. Our door stood beside the entrance to a hairdressing salon. It looked weird, but it was the most affordable place Mum could find. I helped carry boxes labelled 'JD' up to my new room. A sudden wave of loneliness hit me as I sat down and began to unpack. I busied myself to occupy my mind.

We were exhausted by the time all the boxes and furniture had been moved so we ordered pizza. I bit into the gooey slice of heaven as I thought about how I would arrange my room. I found myself coming around to the idea. I also cheered up when I saw the garden. Mum didn't tell me we would have our own garden. Perhaps she wanted to surprise me. Maybe moving to the suburbs wouldn't be so bad after all.

Grabbing the rest of my pizza, I explored the shabby garden. There were overgrown leaves and old spider webs everywhere, but there was a nice picnic table in the middle. Finding a spot that wasn't covered with cobwebs, I carefully perched myself on the edge of the bench.

All of a sudden, I heard a rustling in the bushes. Out came the most beautiful cat I had ever seen with thick, grey fur and smoky, blue eyes. It looked up at me curiously and for a moment the expression looked almost human. I picked off a piece of pepperoni from the slice of pizza in my hand and slowly placed it on the ground. The cat cautiously approached the offering, sniffed at it tentatively, and then ate it greedily. I wondered who its owner was, as it had no collar. It would be great if our garden was some sort of cat hangout. Mum always said we couldn't get a cat because our old apartment was too small. Maybe Mum would let me get one now.

THE NEW GIRL

My first day at Alexandria Primary School was okay. My classmates were helpful and my teacher seemed nice. At lunchtime, I was on my own as I didn't have anyone to hang out with, forgotten by the prefects who had initially been so helpful in the morning. Luckily, I could see that there were sports and games supervised by adults to join in with. Even though a few kids came up to me and asked me for my name, they didn't really stick around so I didn't feel like I had made any new friends. As I walked home later on that day, I spotted the same cat who visited yesterday. There it sat, looking very regal in somebody's front yard. There was another cat sitting beside it – a black one with amber eyes. They both eyed me suspiciously. I walked past them nonchalantly but froze when I heard a strange noise.

"She might be next," a ghostly voice said.

"Shhh..." another voice responded.

I stopped in my tracks, thinking someone was behind me, but all I could see were the cats lounging around. They looked up at me as I passed with narrowed eyes. Surely someone was playing a trick on me.

"JD!"

I spun around and saw a boy I recognised from school across the road. A mop of ginger hair stood out against the dark green bushes behind him.

"Oh, hey, uh... George? I didn't know you lived near me."

"Yeah, I live around the corner from here."

"Oh okay. Um nice seeing you," I said, not really sure what else to say. He seemed to sense my awkwardness and took pity on me.

"Do you wanna hang out?"

Not wanting to ruin my first opportunity to make a friend, I replied, "Yeah, sure. I just need to ask my mum first."

He walked with me to my front door. Luckily, Mum saw the expression on my face willing her not to embarrass me in front of George. She said I could stay out for a little while longer, but I had to be back for dinner at six 'o'clock. We sat outside on the wall and chatted. George was a fun character who had endless, humorous stories to tell me about the kids and teachers at our school. I never had a friend that was a boy before and I almost regretted avoiding the boys at my last school. They only seemed interested in fighting about football. Perhaps I'd been judgemental because George liked some of the same things I did even though he was a boy.

George went to the shop to buy some sweets before heading home. He had asked me to come along, but I didn't think it was a good idea as Mum would be really annoyed if I ate sweets just before dinner. Besides, I had homework to do. Already! We parted ways and I went home with a hop and a skip, feeling pleased that I had made a new friend. At least now I would have someone to talk to and sit with in school.

The next morning, I woke up extra early and extra keen to get to school so I could hang with George before the bell rang. I was disappointed to see that he hadn't arrived yet. I stood alone, hoping he was just late. I sat in class staring at the door whilst the register was being taken, but by nine-thirty he still hadn't arrived. I guessed he must be sick. Maybe I would pop down to his house after school. I'm sure he said he lived at number forty-five, Park Road. I felt slightly embarrassed for looking forward to seeing him so much and decided that I should make more friends. I tried talking to the girl next to me, but she just told me to be quiet. When I tried talking to the boy next to me, he kept pulling funny faces rather than answering. It made me giggle loudly.

"Jaden, is there something funny?"

Caught on the spot, I replied, "No, Miss."

"Get on with your work, please."

I realised that the boy had deliberately tried to get me into trouble when I saw him smirking. Determined not to get into trouble on my first day, I kept my head down for the rest of the lesson.

I tried again in vain to talk to more children at lunchtime, but the girls just huddled in one spot chatting secretively, while most of the boys played basketball noncommittally. I thought their behaviour a little odd. There was a whole different feeling in the air. It wasn't like that the day before. Something was wrong. I skirted the huddles trying to eavesdrop, but when I approached, the huddles became tighter. I thought I heard George's name mentioned in hushed whispers.

Throughout the whole afternoon, certain children were asked to go to the head teacher's office and I became increasingly curious and even slightly uneasy. I watched the clock until home-time, eager to find out why George had not been in.

Stepping onto his doorstep, I nervously pressed the bell. A dishevelled woman with reddened eyes opened the door. Feeling awkward, as this was obviously a bad time, I stammered, "S-s-sorry to disturb you, is George around?"

To my horror, she burst into tears.

"He's gone missing!" she sobbed.

"But I just saw him yesterday," I sputtered in confusion.

"Where is he? Tell me!" she screamed, advancing on me.

"I don't know!"

Frightened, I ran home, but Mum wasn't home yet. I sat in my room and stared at the walls, dumbfounded. Could he really be missing? What if he... I just couldn't even think that for a second. I desperately needed fresh air, so I ran into the garden. The grey cat was there with a ginger cat I had not seen before. The ginger cat came straight towards me and seemed oddly familiar. I petted the cats while trying to figure out where George was and kept seeing his mum's panic-stricken face in my mind. Then, hearing the front door open, I ran into Mum's arms and incoherently told her what had happened. She listened sympathetically while I rambled on.

"Let's hope they find him," she said equally as concerned.

Mum urged me to take a hot bath, while she informed the police.

After eating dinner, the shock of what had happened started to sink in. If he had run away, could I have done anything differently yesterday? It just didn't make sense. He seemed happy enough. It seemed more likely that he had been kidnapped. That was a thought that scared me to death. I was feeling more and more anxious about George going missing so I sat in front of the television trying to drown out my thoughts.

After a while, I began to drift off. Normally Mum would tell me to go to bed if I fell asleep on the settee, but I noticed that she was being especially nice to me tonight. As I dozed, a loud knock disrupted my fitful dreams and I nearly jumped out of my seat. The police arrived with a multitude of questions. Where did you last see George? What were you doing? Did he seem upset? I felt like every answer I gave was useless and I desperately wanted to be helpful. I couldn't help feeling that they were disappointed with my answers.

It was on the news that evening. The disappearance of George was discussed as well as another child who had gone missing recently. I knew that people went missing all the time, but this was scary because it was a lot closer to home, and they had both occurred in the same area.

"Until this is sorted out, you come straight home after school," Mum commanded resolutely.

Well, that wouldn't be difficult, considering the fact that I had no friends.

Despite the shock of George disappearing and the wave of gossip that followed, life went on as usual. Weirdly, it made me more popular all of a sudden. Everyone had found out that I was the last person from school to have seen him. I wasn't sure if I enjoyed this popularity caused by a missing child. Making friends as a result of someone else's misfortune didn't seem right. I felt guilty somehow. I felt dirty.

The girls I had seen chatting the other day included me in their group and even the boys talked to me, but mostly to ask questions about George. After being bombarded with questions, I wondered if it was better to be a 'nobody' after all.

The week dragged on. There was still no word of what had happened to George. Less people approached me at school. I had become old news and so had George unfortunately.

STRANGE EVENTS

I had become friendly with a local girl named Freya. She was home-schooled, but Mum had met her mum in the park by chance one weekend. Since then, they had come over for dinner a couple of times and we had gone to hers. She had brilliant-blue eyes and a mop of curly, brown bedraggled hair. I sometimes wondered if she even owned a brush.

"Hey, Snot Face," she called out. "Stop daydreaming and pass the crisps."

"Okay, Pizza Face," I said as I passed her the bowl. Freya's parents were out of town and Mum had agreed on a sleepover. I paused the movie to use the bathroom and Freya switched to normal television as she waited.

"Oh my God! There's another missing kid!"

"What?" I shouted as I ran back into the living room.

A photograph of a brown-skinned child with large, brown eyes and black, plaited hair took up the whole screen. We both stared at it in disbelief. They still had no idea who or what happened to them and a curfew had been imposed. We couldn't watch the rest of the movie after that and there was no need for a scary story that night. We were scared enough. We set up the sofa bed and tried to sleep.

Scratching.

I woke up to the sound of scratching. It was coming from the garden door. Pushing through my fear, I convinced myself that it was probably an animal. I pulled the curtain aside but didn't see anything. When a face appeared I almost screamed but managed to stop myself in time. It was a tabby cat with big, brown eyes which looked oddly sad. Feeling sorry for it, I open the door and let it come inside. It gingerly stepped in and came up to me. I knelt down to pet it.

"Hey there. Haven't seen you before," I whispered.

"What's going on?" Freya mumbled sleepily.

"Oh, nothing. Just checking out this cat."

"What's with all these cats I've been seeing recently?"

I was about to say that it was normal to see loads of cats when I remembered a news item the other day about concerns over feral cats roaming the area. This cat didn't have a collar, but it certainly didn't look feral. Reluctantly, I nudged the cat towards the garden door, closed it, and headed back to the sofa bed.

The next morning, Mum and I walked Freya home. Mum popped into a shop across the road while I chatted to Freya on her doorstep. She seemed really keen to get inside so I said a quick goodbye. As the front door clicked shut behind her, I suddenly had a really bad feeling. A prickling sensation crept down my neck. An indistinguishable, strangled gargle escaped from my lips when a cat jumped out of a bush unexpectedly. I immediately felt foolish for being so easily spooked and looked around hoping nobody had seen. It was just another cat. This one was white, apart from some black patches on its nose and paws with gleaming, green eyes. They looked straight at me.

"Help me."

I looked around startled, wondering who or what said that.

"Can you hear me?"

It sounded like it was coming from the direction of the cat. Then it suddenly ran off.

"JD? You were off in your own world. Everything okay?" Mum asked, with concern in her eyes as she approached me.

"I'm not sure."

"Maybe you're coming down with something. Let's get you home."

Zombie-like, I numbly followed Mum back home. I turned around every minute or so feeling haunted by voices. Maybe I was losing my mind. It had happened to me before. Surely only crazy people heard voices? I should probably talk to Mum, but she might just brush it off. Or it could go the complete opposite way; she might get really worried and drag me off to the doctor.

Once home, I plonked myself on my bed and absently fiddled with my grandmother's ring, turning it around on my finger. Suddenly, out of nowhere, a flickering light appeared beside me. The light turned into a shape of a woman. To my shock, it was Grandma.

"Don't be afraid, it's only me."

"Grandma? Is it really you?" I asked disbelievingly.

"Yes, it is. Search your heart and feel the truth of my words."

I didn't know how I knew, but somehow I did. It was really her speaking to me.

"I miss you," I choked out, my voice suddenly thick with emotion.

"I miss you, too, but they need your help, JD. Use the power inside of you." Her voice became fainter. "I love you very much."

Before I had a chance to say I loved her too, she disappeared. I couldn't be imagining things. Deep down inside, I knew it was real. I looked down at her ring. It glowed eerily like it was full of life; full of some kind of unearthly power. What power did she mean by the power inside of me? I needed to find out who needed my help.

After having a long think, I hadn't really solved anything. I would have to be patient, but it was really frustrating. I realised that hours had passed and I hadn't eaten since breakfast. I made a peanut butter sandwich and planted myself in front of the television. There was yet another news bulletin. A feeling of dread passed through me. Please don't tell me another child... My heart sank as the news presenter announced that another child had gone missing whilst walking home from school. When I saw a photograph of the unfortunate child, something just clicked. It was like the missing pieces of a jigsaw snapped together. I gasped, unable to breathe. No. It couldn't be. It didn't make any sense! A face with a patchy complexion and gleaming, green eyes bored into mine from the screen. I had just seen a cat with that exact same eye colour! Also, the other day a brown-eyed child went missing, and soon after, I saw a brown-eyed tabby cat. And George! The blue-eyed ginger! And I remember seeing a blue-eyed boy on a missing poster a while back! Could he be the grey cat? I also wondered about the black cat. How could this be? Could it just be a coincidence? Not when I counted the voices too. Something was happening, but I wasn't sure what.

"Oh my God, JD! You look like you've just seen a ghost!" Mum exclaimed.

I sat mutely for a few seconds, and then managed to reply stiffly,

"Another child went missing."

"Oh no! They have to find the people who are doing this. You are not to go anywhere alone from now on." she said firmly.

"But what about school?"

"I'll take you. Do you understand, JD?"

"Yes, Mum," I said numbly, knowing there was no way I could avoid going out on my own. Mum had work. I had school.

I closed the front door behind me and looked around. Mum had gone food shopping and I made the excuse that I wasn't feeling well, so I wouldn't have to come along. After repeatedly assuring Mum that I wouldn't let any strangers in, she left to go.

The sky dimmed as rain clouds gathered overhead. I hoped that Mum had brought her umbrella. As for me, I had my rain jacket on. I walked towards the park, hoping to spot more cats roaming the streets, but I couldn't see a soul. It seemed strange, devoid of both humans and animals. I guess I had chosen the worst time to look. Who goes for a walk when it's raining? The place seemed like a ghost town. I could feel my courage dissipating so I quickly made my way back and made sure to hide the wet jacket and shoes before Mum returned.

Mum arrived home shortly after, finding me dozing on the settee which corroborated my story about not feeling well. Satisfied that she didn't suspect anything, I went to my room and wrote down everything that had gone on in the last month. Some questions still remained: How were the missing children picked, and how had they *transformed*?

That night, I logged on to my laptop and searched for all I could about humans turning into creatures. All these strange articles about shape-shifting and werewolves came up. Then again, if children really could turn into cats, then maybe ghouls, goblins, and ghosts were real too. Maybe I believed in ghosts after all. Maybe even vampires and werewolves were real too. Who knew? Some sources mentioned witchcraft. Well, something like that must be involved as it certainly wasn't normal for children to turn into cats. How did these things exist? The world definitely was an intriguing place full of secrets and darkness.

After hours of searching, I turned off the laptop in frustration as I felt like I hadn't gotten anywhere near solving this riddle. My head exploded with useless information. I felt exhausted. I had school tomorrow and I desperately needed to sleep. I brushed my teeth, washed my face, and put my pyjamas on. I went to say goodnight to Mum. She held me in a fierce embrace and told me that she loved me. I think the missing children had scared her. It made us both afraid realising that it could happen to anyone, even me. I truly was alone when it came to this. I couldn't ask Mum or the authorities for help. No one would believe me.

FINDING THE TRUTH

Mum bringing me to school just wasn't practical. I waited by the front door as she looked for her travel card. I knew that I was going to be late.

"Mum! Can I just go to school?"

"I won't be a minute."

"I can go by myself. It's broad daylight. Nothing will happen to me. I'll run if I see anything suspicious." I waited for a response. No answer.

"Mum! I need to go!"

Exasperated, she agreed, "Okay, JD. You go ahead. I'll catch up with you. Remember not to speak to any strangers!"

Knowing Mum, there was no way she would catch up with me.

"Okay, Mum. I love you," I said, giving her a quick peck on the cheek. Sometimes I wondered how we functioned at all.

I broke into a medium-paced jog and was making progress until I was only five minutes away. When a black shadow darted in front of me, I abruptly stopped in my tracks, steadying myself on a nearby wall. I saw a black cat totter towards an abandoned house and just before it entered, its amber eyes looked back at me for an instant. The cat flap in the dilapidated, wooden door swung shut. Another cat followed suit. This one I recognised – the grey one. I decided to follow them...

Squeezing my way through splintered wood around the back of the house, I cautiously approached a closed window. I strained my ears, yet I heard nothing. Crouched low, I tried to find another window. Eventually, I found an open window. I carefully pushed it up. My heart pounded as it creaked open. I removed my shoes leaving them in a nearby bush and slowly climbed in. Extremely aware of any noise I made, I gently stepped further inside. Noise was coming from the cellar. I could hear talking. I inched closer to the door, which was slightly ajar.

"The familiars are here now," a female voice declared. She sounded slightly older than me.

"It was silly choosing familiars from this area. Now there's a search for them."

"How could anyone know they used to be children?"

I couldn't believe my ears. I took one step closer, hoping to hear more. It was true! These cats were no ordinary cats. The floorboards suddenly creaked under my weight.

"What's that?"

"I'll go and check," a boy's voice responded.

"Yes, George, you check," another voice agreed.

Stepping back, I stood stiffly behind the door. Out popped a ginger cat who found me immediately.

"George?"

He stared at me intensely in response and then walked towards the window. There it stood until I followed. I realised he wanted me to escape. He was helping me. Not wanting to get caught, I climbed back out of the window.

"Stay safe," a faint voice whispered.

I turned my head as fast as I could, but George was gone. Had he just spoken to me? Yes. I couldn't be 'hearing voices'. I heard an actual voice and I was pretty certain it sounded like George. Perhaps I could sense his thoughts or maybe he was actually speaking. I guessed that I would find out soon enough. I hurried off to school after retrieving my shoes from the bush, knowing full well that I would be late. Surely, Mum had phoned the school, as I would have been late anyway after the travel card drama.

That evening I was restless. I wanted to go back to the house but was worried that those people would be there. I waited until Mum was snoring away and nestled in front of the television watching her favourite show. I snuck out the door and made my way to the abandoned house. The window was open just as I had left it. I located the cellar. Not detecting any sound, I switched my torch on and slowly walked down the dusty staircase. What I saw confirmed my worst fears. There was some kind of symbol that looked like a pentagram painted on the ground. It looked like some kind of ritual had taken place. Familiars and pentagrams could mean only one thing according to my internet search.

Witches.

Luckily, I had left the front door open when I left. I knew it was risky, but it was the only way I could sneak out and return without being caught by Mum. Mum was still dozing peacefully on the sofa, so I headed to my room to mull over everything.

How do I combat witches? How can I save the 'cat' children? I had no idea. I looked down at Grandma's ring and started twirling it around my finger, hoping it would focus me somehow. Instead, something strange happened. It shimmered and glowed with a luminescence that was just too unreal to be real. The room became fuzzy...

I was watching my baby cousin at my Grandma's funeral. I heard my aunties talking in hushed tones.

"What should we do with all of these herbs and potions? And what about the grimoire?"

"I don't know. Just throw them away. I don't want them. They make me feel uncomfortable."

"You always denied your heritage."

"Not my heritage."

"Okay, I'll keep them. She would want us to."

The image blurred and I was still sitting on my bed. Why did Grandma have potions? Was she a witch? And what was a grimoire? I had been nine years old when Grandma died and that memory had replayed itself like it was only yesterday. Not only did it bring back this longing to see Grandma again, but I also had a multitude of questions to ask. Did Auntie Kay still have Grandma's things? Did Mum know Grandma's secrets?

"Mum? Wake up."

Mum groggily opened her eyes. "Oh my. I must have dozed off. What time is it?"

"Nine 'o'clock."

"Why didn't you wake me?"

"I didn't want to disturb you. You're obviously tired."

"Sorry, my love."

"It's okay Mum. Actually, I have a question. Can we visit Auntie Kay? We haven't seen any family for a long time." Mum's face darkened as she had not spoken to Auntie Kay in quite some time. Not since Grandma's funeral.

"I don't think she wants to see us, JD."

"Let me call her or something. Why aren't you guys talking anyway?"

"She made crazy accusations that just

weren't true"

"Like what, Mum?"

"I don't want to talk about it. I just think it's a bad idea."

Seeing that Mum was visibly agitated, I dropped the subject and formulated a plan of my own. While Mum readied herself for bed, I looked at her phone hoping to find Auntie Kay's number. I knew her password but didn't know that she had removed her number. I remembered that Mum had a diary with addresses in it years ago. Maybe it was in one of the boxes that still lay unpacked in the attic.

"JD, why are you going up there now?" Mum called up.

"Oh, I left one of my boxes up there," I lied.

There was no response from Mum, so I continued up to the attic. At least a dozen boxes had not been unpacked and all of them were not labelled. Going through each box one by one was a painful process. Some were heavy and piled on top of others. I was down to the last couple of boxes when I dropped one. The tape loosened and all the contents fell out.

"JD, are you alright?"

"Yes, Mum."

I could hear Mum's footsteps getting louder when I spotted the diary. I quickly grabbed it and tucked it under my top as Mum walked in.

"Why would any of your things be in these boxes," she said, gesturing to the kitchen utensils and VHS tapes scattered about the floor.

"I thought I saw something to watch."

"Why would you want to watch old videotapes? Didn't I throw the old VHS player away years ago?"

"Well, why did we keep the videos then, Mum?" I said cheekily, hoping it would be enough to distract her.

"Okay, don't get smart with me. Clean up this mess and get yourself to bed. You have school, remember?"

As the buzzer went at the end of the school day, I was filled with a nervous excitement. Some of it was positive because I could finally speak to Auntie Kay again; some of it was apprehension. I wasn't sure if she would answer the questions I had to ask. As suspected, Mum couldn't collect me due to work. I quickly rushed home because I didn't have any credit and wanted to use the landline phone before Mum arrived home. The moment I stepped in, I picked up the phone and dialled the number. The more it rang unanswered, the more my heart sank. I needed answers now. My heartbeat quickened when I heard a click.

"Hello?" A tiny voice answered.

"Hi, is that Evie?"

"Um, yeah. Why? Who's this?"

"It's your cousin, JD."

I heard a sharp intake of breath.

"Oh my God! Never thought I'd speak to you again. Mummy tried to call Auntie Judy loads of times, but there's always no answer."

"Well, I need to speak to your mum now. It's really important, Evie."

"Oh no, did something bad happen?"

"No. Yes. I don't know," I replied confused.

"What's going on?" she said, worry creeping into her voice.

"Can you please get Auntie Kay?"

Sensing my urgency, she said, "Okay, I'll get her."

I took a deep breath, trying to calm my nerves as I waited.

"JD? Is that you?" a frantic voice answered.

"Yes, Auntie Kay. It's me."

"What is it? Is it my sister? Is she okay? This silence has gone too far!"

"I know Auntie." Even though I wanted to help resolve family issues, I had a more urgent issue on my mind. "I need your help."

"Tell me JD, is Jude okay?"

"Yes, she's fine. It's about something else. It's about Grandma. Um, was she a... Did she ever... What I'm trying to say is..." I stammered.

"I think I know what you're asking. Yes, Grandma was a witch, JD. That's why your mum won't talk to me. Why are you asking me this? How did you know?"

"I saw something. Some kind of vision or hallucination." The line went silent. "Auntie?"

"You've got it, JD. The gift." Unsure of what that meant, I remained silent.

"You need the grimoire to help guide you. Tell Judy I'm coming down."

"She doesn't know about this call, Auntie Kay."

We continued talking for about half an hour as I explained what had happened to the children. She gasped in shock and horror. She explained that familiars should not be children, but trapped souls who offered themselves. Their souls would be given a vessel, usually cats, but sometimes other animals. An animal that was close to death was the preferred method. She added that trapping people against their will would require powerful magic. Only dark magic used such methods. Unfortunately, I had to cut our conversation short, as I could hear the jingle of keys just outside the front door.

SECRETS AND LIES

Mum stood agape at the front door but had enough sense to greet Evie like a decent aunty would. True to her word, Aunty Kay had come. I noticed that Mum didn't greet her sister the same way as she had Evie, but I gave both Auntie Kay and Evie a hug. I brought my cousin to my room, while Mum and Auntie Kay stayed in the sitting room. Serious talks ahead I guessed. A short while later, I overheard crying and raised voices. I wanted to be a fly on the wall, rather than with my cousin at that moment.

"Oh yeah, Mum said to give this to you," said Evie as she handed me what looked like a really old journal.

"What is it?" I asked confused.

"I think it's Grandma's diary."

I turned the leather-bound book around, inspecting the cover, and leafed through it briefly. On the first page, there was some writing in neat cursive script which read, *Elspeth's grimoire.*

Now I knew what a grimoire was. This is what Auntie Kay said I needed to read. Deciding to look at it when I was alone, I placed it in my bedside cabinet drawer. I probably wouldn't show Mum any time soon. Or ever. The voices from the living room became louder.

"No. I don't want to hear it."

"But you're denying the truth. Ma knew you couldn't handle it after dad died. You took it so hard. You were in pieces."

"I won't hear this nonsense."

The more I heard the more worried and

disappointed I felt. It looked like they wouldn't resolve their issues tonight. My aunt appeared at my bedroom door and announced,

"Evie we're leaving."

"But we just got here!"

"Evie," Auntie Kay commanded. "Now."

And just like that, they were gone.

Mum was standing, looking out the window. Tears were flowing down her face.

"Mum? Are you ok?"

"Why did you call her?"

As much as I didn't want to see Mum upset, I was glad that Auntie Kay hadn't told her why I had called in the first place. I didn't think Mum would take it well.

"I thought it would help," I explained honestly as I hugged her. It was a real shame they hadn't worked out their problems. I could see Mum just couldn't accept some things. Maybe she hadn't seen Grandma do magic. Maybe I could somehow convince her one day. I told Mum to relax while I made something that resembled food for dinner. I placed sandwiches and a cup of tea in front of Mum on the coffee table and we sat in silence as we ate. Mum called it a night soon after.

In my room, I eagerly retrieved the grimoire and started reading. It was filled with herbal remedies, potions, and spells. It also had information about our family tree. Grandma was descended from a witch mother and a non-witch father. The 'gift' was passed down to her, but not her daughters. That meant Mum and Auntie Kay didn't have it. I don't think Aunt Maureen had either. I wondered if Evie had shown any signs of it, but assumed that if she had, the grimoire would be hers. So, if I was having visions, then I must have the 'gift'. I just wish I had Grandma to guide me. I looked down at Grandma's ring and then it happened. A vision.

Grandma was sitting on the bed beside me. She pointed to the grimoire. It's time," she said gently.

"I can't do it alone."

"You have to try."

The vision faded as rapidly as it had appeared, but I think I understood what it meant. I think Grandma was telling me to read and learn. She was still guiding me, even though she had physically gone.

I looked at the first few spells and remedies in the book and realised that I could easily attain some of the ingredients and components. I just had to make sure I recited the rhyming words to invoke the spell. I wanted to try one out tomorrow if I could. I would need to raid the kitchen cupboard for the ingredients and bind them together. Some of the spells didn't require ingredients, just an object. Maybe I would try the flower spell. All that was required was a drop of water and sunlight. It sounded simple enough:

Listen to the words that I cite
You will stand tall and bright
To you, one more breath I give
I command you, blossom, to live

I was up at the crack of dawn on a school day. Getting up this early was certainly unheard of for me. I drowsily tumbled out of bed, got a glass of water, and located a withered flower in the garden. After the fifth try of reciting the words, I gave up. Disheartened, I got ready for school. I put the grimoire in my bag and left. A forlorn-looking Mum bid me farewell as we parted ways by the bus stop.

Despite me telling my friends I just wanted to be alone, they all surrounded me, asking what was wrong. I just said I missed my aunty and my cousin. I hadn't realised that my feelings were that transparent. There was me thinking I was hiding everything so well. Even though I truly did miss them, I just wanted to be alone to try that spell one more time. In the middle of French lesson, I realised what may have gone wrong. I think the flower had to be in direct sunlight. I wasn't sure why I hadn't thought of that before.

Instead of going straight home like I had promised Mum, I went home via the park. I found lots of wilted flowers that I could use. Once I was ready to cast the spell, I found a secluded spot. I recited the words to no avail. I recited the words once more and I held my breath as I waited. Just as I was about to give up, time seemed to slow down. I could hear each breath I took and each beat of my heart as if it was amplified. Before my very eyes, the flower regained its vibrant, yellow colour and stood tall and upright. It seemed to sing with energy and a renewed spirit. Despite my initial joy at discovering my newfound powers, the current problem still hung over me like deadweight.

Fortunately, Mum couldn't question me about where I had been as her shift at work had changed. She was nervous about the disappearances and wanted to ensure my safety, but her unsympathetic boss had other employees with children and couldn't shut things down so parents could go home early. We needed the money after the huge deposit Mum had to pay when we moved house and she wouldn't let me do a paper round or anything at the moment. The sooner I could solve this, the better. Then I could have a bit more freedom.

Fishing the grimoire out of my school bag, I carefully searched through the book in the hope that I could find something to help. I came across a masking spell that might help in days to come, but I needed something more powerful.

The front door opened.

"JD? You home?"

"Yes, Mum."

Mum walked into my room and just in the nick of time, I slid the book behind me. She gave me a perplexed look, probably wondering why I was sitting on the floor with nothing to read or do.

"I was about to start my homework," I quickly blurted out. I reached for my backpack, which happened to be right next to me, to retrieve my school books.

"Oh okay. We're having pasta for dinner tonight."

She came toward me to kiss me on my forehead. Normally she did that straight away, but she probably had a lot on her mind, so I quickly shoved my bag behind me to cover the grimoire.

"Love you, Mum."

"Love you too."

I think Mum was relieved to see me safe and at home. When Mum left to cook, I quickly reached for the grimoire, accidentally dropping it. It opened as it fell and I tried to flip back to the masking spell. Then strangely, as if an invisible force moved it, the book opened on the same page again. *Trapped Souls*. This was it. Somehow the grimoire knew what I was looking for. The ritual described involved a sacrifice of some kind. I wasn't sure what kind of sacrifice though. I felt nauseous reading it. No matter how uncomfortable I felt, I knew that I must do this.

Attaining all the necessary ingredients would be the next dilemma. I made a list of everything I needed, determined to get them tomorrow. I had to get salt, chalk to draw a pentagram, and nepeta cataria (catnip). I would have to learn the incantation:

I call on Witch Queen Hecate
Pass your power through me
Free the souls trapped in these forms
Return the bodies from which they were torn
Undo the cursed evil Mark
Reverse the spell that is dark

FACING THE ENEMY

Mum had a good start this morning. She walked me all the way to school and even watched me walk to the gate. We waved goodbye to each other. As soon as she disappeared around the corner, I snuck away in the opposite direction and hoped that none of the teachers had seen me. Taking out my hand-drawn map, I headed to the closest pet shop that I had found on the internet last night. Lost, I asked several people for directions. I was so afraid that I would get caught. Around an hour later, I managed to locate it. Opening time was ten, which meant I had to wait another fifteen minutes. I had to resort to waiting in somebody's front yard crouched low behind a wall. I felt silly like I was playing hide-and-seek. When it was ten, I returned to see someone opening up. I stepped behind her.

"Oh my gosh! You gave me the fright of my life!" a middle-aged woman with silver hair shrieked.

"Oh sorry, I didn't mean to scare you."

"Aren't you supposed to be at school?"

"Um... I'm homeschooled," I lied. I was starting to worry about how easily I managed to lie these days and how trusting people were.

"Oh yeah? I hear lots of people are doing that now. What can I do for you?"

"I'm looking for some catnip," I explained.

"Ah, well, I've got catnip sticks."

"Do you have any fresh catnip at all?"

"Only out back, but it's not for sale yet."

"Would you mind if I had a look at it to make

a comparison?"

She looked at me with confusion in her eyes, wondering why I would need to look at catnip.

"It's for a research project."

"Okay, I guess that wouldn't be a problem."

"Thanks."

She disappeared down the dark and narrow corridor and returned holding a clay pot containing a very standard-looking plant. At that moment another customer came in. I hastily grabbed a handful of leaves and shoved it into my pocket. I hurriedly made my way to the door and shouted a thank you. Not wanting to draw attention to myself, I power-walked back towards home. I hoped the pet shop lady wouldn't notice that I had stolen anything. It was for a good cause after all. At home, I got the salt and the grimoire.

I took a deep breath as I approached the creepy house. I really hoped I was up to the task. I wasn't feeling as confident as I had earlier. Going around the side of the building as before, I found the open window again. I carefully tiptoed towards the cellar. I strained my ears and heard nothing. Once I got down the stairs, I saw evidence of more witchcraft having been practised. There were candles, symbols, chicken feathers, and a few objects that I didn't recognise scattered around. It smelled awful too. I wondered where the witches were.

Finding a clear spot towards one corner of the room, I proceeded to draw a pentagram with chalk. I went over the lines with salt and put the catnip in the middle along with my grimoire. I sat in the middle of the pentagram and practised the incantation. The whole thing felt surreal, like something out of a movie.

When I felt ready I decided to start summoning the trapped souls:

Lost souls, I summon thee
So that you might be free

The flame on the candle flickered and grew larger. To my surprise, a cobalt-coloured smoke arose and escaped up the stairs. I sat frozen on the spot, not knowing what else to do, and waited with bated breath. As the minutes stretched on, the back of my neck prickled uncomfortably due to the unmistakable feeling that I was being watched. I took a deep breath. I turned around slowly and in the shadows, two green eyes gleamed. Another cat – as black as a shadow – unexpectedly leaped out. Then I heard paws softly pattering down the stairs. First, the grey cat appeared. It was followed by the tabby and lastly, the ginger cat, George.

They automatically went to their spots on the pentagram without breaking the salt barrier. They seemed to know what they were there for. I recited the incantation:

I call on Witch Queen Hecate
Pass your power through me
Free the souls trapped in these forms
Return the bodies from which they were torn
Undo the cursed evil Mark
Reverse the spell that is dark

A light breeze began to waft around and I felt a surge of power gathering strength deep in my gut, but as soon as it began, it disappeared as quickly. Something didn't feel right. I took another deep breath, planning to recite the incantation again. I could no longer get the words out, no matter how hard I tried.

A high-pitched cackle stopped me in my tracks.

"Not so fast false witch!" a shrill voice screamed. Another voice squealed with delight.

"Fresh meat!"

"We haven't had fresh meat for a while."

I tried to respond, but my lips wouldn't move. My arms were being bound by a rope, which twisted around my wrists like a slithering snake.

"Turn her into a cat!"

"She'll be bound forever and no one will ever know!" the other witch exclaimed gleefully.

Five witches revealed themselves. They looked just like normal teenage girls at first, but when their eyes met mine, they glowed with an unnatural light. They were devoid of emotion. Their faces appeared feral, replacing anything human. Their cold, empty eyes stared through me like I was invisible. They pierced my body like icicles. I began to lose hope. One witch swiped the air with her hand, sending the cats hurtling to the other side of the room. The witches took their places on each vertex of the pentagram and started to chant in unison:

Bind this soul in the body of...

I looked around desperately, scared to death of being trapped in a cat's body. I tried to make as much noise as I could, but all that came out was a mumbled, incoherent sound. I screamed silently. Somebody help me! Grandma, where are you?

Wind swirled around, encircling the coven and me. All I could see was debris and dust. I choked on the putrid air. My eyes stung and tears ran down my face. I heard cats screeching agonisingly. The wind finally subsided and I saw the cats attempting to attack the coven. I quickly looked around for something to sever my bonds. Thankfully, I found a piece of jagged broken glass. Accidentally cutting myself in the process, I freed myself. At that moment I realised where I had gone wrong with the spell. I needed to make a sacrifice.

As the cats distracted them with all their might, I closed the gaps in the pentagram with salt. Praying that my deep cut was enough of a sacrifice, I stood in the middle and recited the words with a renewed vigour. The cats returned to their spots and a whirlwind surrounded us. An ethereal sphere encircled us, forming a protective barrier and an invisible force seemed to hold the witches back. I closed my eyes, drawing on all my inner strength as I repeated the spell over and over again. So lost in my own world that after some time, the only noise I could hear was the sound of my own heavy breathing. My eyes were still shut tight because I was still afraid to open them.

"It's okay, JD. You did it!"

I recognised that voice. Before I even opened my eyes, I said, "George?"

And there he was sitting before me.

"Oh my god," I sobbed.

Five other familiar faces sat around me. I remembered seeing these faces on news reports. George looked exactly the same as the day before he went missing. He wore the same ghastly white and orange, striped top and dark, denim jeans. His ginger tuft of hair was still a wild bird's nest. There were tears in his blue eyes. We all just sat there in shock, wildly dishevelled and feeling as though we had just fought a war.

Battle weary and consumed with our own jumbled-up mixed emotions, we had almost forgotten the evil coven of witches who had started all of this. What had previously appeared to be young girls were now shrivelled up old prunes. Skeletal disjointed dolls lay on the ground with white wispy hair on their dry, balding skulls.

"This was our last chance to live again."

"We can't survive for much longer," a weak voice rattled.

"Don't listen to them, JD. They used our life essence to regain their youth. Our souls survived inside of these cats."

Five lifeless cats lay beside each child like an empty vessel. Used and drained of life. What had occurred started to sink in.

"You don't deserve to survive. You were willing to condemn innocent children to a living hell."

Their ragged breaths came out in wheezing gasps as their bodies decomposed. They shrivelled up until there was nothing left. Their brittle remains began to crumble and crack until they turned to dust and disintegrated. We all sat in silence holding our breath, hoping that the coven wouldn't return, and hoping that they were truly gone.

After quite some time, the dark-haired boy said, "I want to go home."

"What are we going to say to our parents," the girl with the plaited hair asked.

"They wouldn't believe us."

"And the police?"

"I'm going to tell the truth."

We all rose, determination in our movements, but wobbly. I guessed that they hadn't walked on two legs for some time. We huddled together.

"Whatever you say, your parents will be happy to see you."

Five exhausted and grubby, mud-stained children walked with me to my house, where I found Mum frantically crying her eyes out, thinking that I had been kidnapped. Well, she wasn't far off. She called the police to let them know that I had found the missing children in an abandoned house on the way to school...

The next few days had been utter mayhem. The police had questioned everyone involved countless times and all they had gotten was very confused, vague accounts of what had happened. Five elderly women and five young women were being searched for. We wished that we could have saved them the effort of looking for the suspects, but there was nothing that we could do. I was so glad when all the media attention, the police involvement, and queries from baffled parents died down.

The day before I was due to return to school, Grandma decided to pay us a visit. She materialised at exactly the right moment. Mum had broken down in tears as she knew deep in her heart that Grandma's death had almost destroyed her. Grandma told her to resolve things with Aunty Kay and to encourage my abilities as much as she could. That evening, Mum called her sister and we were invited to their house for Christmas this year and I couldn't wait. We could finally be a proper family.

EPILOGUE

I pressed the bell at number forty-five. A cheerful boy with chaotic, orange hair opened the door. For some reason, he was now wearing a ghastly green and white, striped top. I had never felt happier to see such a horrible shade of green, despite how much my eyes ached.

"Are you ready, George?"

"Of course I am. Can't wait to go back to school!" he said excitedly.

"Never thought I'd see the day when we actually looked forward to going to school."

"You would be surprised how much I missed school after being stuck in a cat's body," he chuckled. I couldn't believe he had managed to retain his sense of humour after all that had happened.

"I'm so glad you're back, George."

"I'm so glad you're a witch, JD."

I punched him playfully on the arm. I didn't care that everyone teased us for being friends. I didn't care that he was a boy. To me, he was my best friend.

ABOUT THE AUTHOR

As a young child, L. F. Gobin was an avid reader who often created her own stories and illustrations. Later on, she developed an interest in writing poetry, songs, and novels. After years of reading fantasy stories, she decided to write her own children's novella.

JD's character partially reflects her own inquisitive personality, and the storyline of Missing was influenced by moving from central London to leafy suburbia. She was inspired by a nearby abandoned house and the neighbours' cats...

Printed in Great Britain
by Amazon